# The Pocket Anthology

by the Write Here at Dundonald Castle
Writing Group

Write Here
AT DUNDONALD CASTLE

FRIENDS OF DUNDONALD CASTLE SCIO (SC031541)

# The Pocket Anthology



ISBN: 978- 1-7399088-7-4

1371 - 2021

FRIENDS OF

Dundonald Castle

SC 031541

650 YEARS

# Introduction

Dundonald Castle sits atop a volcanic plug right in the heart of the 3 Ayrshire counties. It boasts incredible views right out across Ayrshire and the Clyde. The history of Dundonald Castle hill spans at least 3500 years and has seen many fortifications over its long life including Bronze Age roundhouses, an Iron Age Hillfort, a possible timber motte and bailey castle, a possible kite-shaped castle of enceinte and finally a royal towerhouse. Royal Dundonald Castle is renowned for being the Cradle of the Stewart Dynasty which lasted for 343 years starting with our very own King Bob (Robert II), who was grandson to Robert the Bruce. Dundonald Castle also has familial ties with the Wallaces, Cochranes and Montgomeries.

Friends of Dundonald Castle SCIO (SC031541) manage the site on daily basis through a partnership agreement with Historic Environment Scotland (SC045925). FoDC are committed to exciting and engaging people in their heritage, bringing life back to the Castle and delivering a first-class visitor experience for all.

FoDC are a heritage-based charity who are very focused on being at the heart of their community. As part of their community engagement, they facilitate several regular community groups including the 'Write Here at Dundonald Castle Writing Group'.

This group began as a couple of workshops that were hosted by our Writer in Residence, Lorraine Johnston, during the summer of 2021. These workshops quickly and naturally transformed into a regular writing group. Many of the members of this group had a dream of becoming a published writer, and so the Pocket Anthology idea was born. This is the first anthology to be published by FoDC and we hope that it inspires other writers, well practiced or just starting out, to pick up their pens and explore the amazing world of writing.

To find out more about the history and archaeology of Dundonald Castle, our charity, or our groups, please visit our website (www.dundonaldcastle.org.uk) and social media channels.

# Foreword

When people say they would like to write, I always encourage them to do so. Sometimes, those people take a long time to start, waiting for the *right* time or until they *have* the time.

However, once they start to write, they begin an exciting journey. When that writing gets pushed out into the world, it becomes a thrilling journey that can be shared with others, hopefully leaving an impression.

This collection of stories is the work from six new writers, after only three months of joining their first writing workshop at 'Write here at Dundonald Castle'.

One story has been written by me, leading the way to show what can happen when you push your words out there, for others to read.

Lorraine Johnston

Resident Writer at Dundonald Castle
www.writerlorrainejohnston.com

# Contents

# The Last Theft
## by Paul J Brunton

I've stolen from the best and they never knew a thing. What I do demands courage and skill. Have I ever stolen from the poor?

Yes.

I stole from the poorest of them all on the Mountain of Skulls.

Picking a pocket is never simply about the physical act, it requires attention to detail, skill, and imagination. It requires people, disguises, confusion, and focus. It demands courage and perseverance.

The sun is sinking into the hills and the weeping women in their black gowns of mourning are returning to their homes to eat, drink, smoke, and sleep, knowing there's nothing more they can do. He won't die tonight, but he'll need someone with him, to share his pain.

A friend.

I am an Elder of the Tribe, Zachariah, a rich merchant, and the guards will always defer to the privacy of family and close friends, they are human too. This evening I am the last of them, the mourners, the watchers, and protectors. It's a clear sky, it'll get cold tonight, but at least I'll be warm in this poncho gifted to me by a shepherd a long time ago.

He, up there on that cross, wears only a grey linen loin cloth round his waist. If there's anything hidden, I'll know exactly where to reach in the folds. I won't do it straight away; this has never been my style.

I drink a little water, rip away the unleavened bread with my teeth and chew on some dried fruit. I have never been caught; I stand undefeated. Since I was a child my father and his brothers taught me all the tricks of the trade. It's in my blood. It's a way of life. It allows me to escape. It's an art form that I have expanded in so many ways.

They place these martyrs and criminals close enough to touch but too high to feed or give them water.

It wouldn't help him anyway; it would just prolong the agony. He's drying up, his breathing is slow and harsh, barely human. Although he's a young man, this begins his third day without water. I have seen birds peck at the eyes of these men today. I have seen these dry hills turned into stinking toilets by those who are mainly here out of morbid curiosity.

Each breath could be his last. I could be the one who shares his final moments. My one duty is to change over the fresh cloths dipped in myrrh and honey and apply them to his wounds, and should he wake, comfort him with gentle and kind words.

Looking around, I force myself to rise like an old arthritic bull and stagger painfully towards that wooden cross where he hangs almost lifeless.

All men and women retain their secrets until their final moments.

As I carefully tend the wounds on his wasted, beautiful body I look up to his thin beard and hollowed eyes that have not opened since morning. For a moment I am struck by the fear that his eyes might suddenly open and look upon me. That it should be him, of all people, who is the first to catch me in the act.

I peel away the cloths from his broken feet and rewrap the fresh linen while breathing in the healing herbs that take me back to my sickly childhood and the women who once tended me. He is awake though he can no longer speak. His body tenses and he lets out a harsh cough, a choke, an almost vomit but there's nothing left inside his belly.

Everyone has a secret. Everyone has something to hide. And so, with him, even him. He's right-handed, I know exactly where it will be.

I reach up, slip my fingers down until I find the hidden furls and steal from him the final secret.

Yes.

Grasping the tiny parcel in my hand I turn, and I run, and I run, I run until I am as far from him as I can be. I run until my ageing shins and my collapsing knees give way and fire burns my lungs. Falling to the ground I fix my hair, my white curls now covered in sweat and sand and gently unfold the vellum, in the dim light.

"To all those who pick the pockets of the innocent shall come the vilest rain. May all your misdeeds come back upon you thrice over. Though I have eyes, I no longer have the strength to see. Let your eyes become my eyes, your breath become mine."

A big brass bell tolls in the distance. Three times then silence. It foretells of dangers, an invading army, or plague, or maybe it's just blowing in the wind that has only now picked up.

I rise from my knees grasping the message tightly in my hand. All that I have done must now be undone.

Ever since that moment, I have spent my life burying and uncovering this message in the sand, and I will not stop until I have given away all my vast fortune. If you should find a gold coin wrapped in vellum, then know that it has come from a thief who is returning his wealth through a love for mankind, then stealing it back before returning it, then stealing it back before returning it.

This is my curse and until I am as poor as the man from whom I stole the secret, I will find no peace.

# A Father's Foy
## by Bea C Clark

A swift flick of the knife and the bream were prepared, guts blindly thrown out to sea. Herring gulls snatched their awaited reward mid-flight. Their chorus of victorious laughs ensued. John had learned much from his father, Per, who had raised him after his wife had died. John sifted through his mind searching his Shetland childhood. He couldn't find her. A quiet pain of the unspoken had lain between father and son. Mother was never discussed.

His father had been a deep-sea whaler who had taken immense pride in his Nordic heritage. He often spoke of traditions and showed his son many long-standing skills. John listened intently, hoping for some whisper of mother. As he smiled reflectively, he cleaned the pocketknife on his sleeve and stirred his sugared tea with its blade. He stared into the toffee-coloured liquid and watched the captured whirlpool disappear. John looked towards his father and the little journal he had kept by his side. John was to read it when it was 'right to do so'.

Meanwhile, John had a task. He was to build his father's foy, a shore fire that took patience and skill to get right and was one of his father's cherished traditions.

"I'll make a foy for you, one your ancestors would be proud of." John said convincingly.

As if knowing the importance of the day, the beach had gifted all he needed. The high spring tide was on the turn and so John got to work. He sunk his father's spade deep into the sand. He dug the pit below the tideline as he gauged the water's fast retreat. He lined it carefully with rocks. With all the natural delights of the shoreline to hand, he lit dried grasses with an old flint and fed the driftwood to the growing flame. With the knife curled inside his knuckles, John carved the peat, peeling layers towards him akin to a pipe smoker preparing a tobacco block. As he rubbed the dross into his palms, he gazed upon their dirt-embedded creases. How alike his hands were to his father's, he thought as he stared into them, through them.

John intensely inhaled the raw awakenings of the aged fuel. He felt that all-encompassing sensation of comfort, of love, glowing like a stomach satisfied by a warm thick soup.

"Home." He sighed, lost momentarily in reminiscence.

He felt the foy was a fitting way to say his goodbye. His father often spoke of foys of the past and the significance of marking farewells.

John sat beside his father and the string-bound journal as he waited patiently for the pyre to turn to a white-hot ash. He arranged the fresh array of seaweeds on the smouldering pit before laying the bream on its green bed. Wild garlic, he'd crushed between two stones, was rubbed into their bellies and another layer of delicate seaweed ribbons covered the feast. The foy was complete.

As he waited, John studied the pocketknife. A single steel blade folded into its handle of dark wood. Its cracks and darkened steel revealed age. It was his now. One of the last few tangible connections to his father. As he rolled the open knife between index fingers and thumbs, he hummed a tune, a melodic Nordic whaling song they'd often sung together.

Perplexed now, John looked at the neck of the blade to a letter 'P', half a heart shape and a faint vertical line. John had not noticed the intricate engraving before. He had watched his father do many tasks with his knife throughout the years: opening envelopes, cutting twine, slicing fruit, yet this was the first time he'd noticed this.

He folded the knife and placed it carefully inside his jacket pocket. Momentarily, he looked towards the now distant sea. He decided it was time to open his father's journal. It felt satisfying to finally open his father's companion yet it felt intrusive too.

John unwound the string and pages flapped in the shore breeze, akin to a fledgling attempting flight. 'British Embassy, Oslo'. His heart began to beat a little faster, his mouth suddenly dry. He caught a glimpse of a small, pressed flower, a pinned white feather, and a Telegram.

NAZI OCCUPATION STOP GONE FISHING STOP MADELINE

It seemed Madeline was her codename in the UK Secret Service. She'd been posted overseas to act as a wireless operator in German-occupied Norway, a task with insurmountable risk. No mention of fear, only a firm sense of duty, to help families escape the regime. Through her writings, he sensed she found solace in this.

John lightly touched the slanted writing with attractive flowing 'f's' and capitals topped by feminine loops and curves. He held the open journal to his nose. He tried to breathe his mother's essence.

‘I tried.’ John read the last of her words. Where the script had abruptly stopped, the familiarity of his father’s hand began.

Per had decided he needed to help too. He couldn’t leave her to do this alone. He’d singlehandedly taken his fishing boat into occupied waters. He had to go.

He was aware the Quisling regime of 1941 had fleets in the North Sea, with the threat of British defeat strong. Regardless, he ventured with hope in his heart to find her. Instead, Per encountered the coastal fringes crowded with starving families desperate to escape Nazi rule. Under darkness and in silence, he piled on-board as many people as he safely could. Heavy-heartedly and with eternally grateful passengers, he sailed towards home. Per enquired about Mary to every single one of them.

“Mary, my mother’s name.” John choked, as a tear broke free. “Why couldn’t you say her name, father?”

Per returned the families to safe waters. The journal revealed Per felt humbled as news of his bravery had spread. Soon a fleet of vessels taxiing between safe and occupied shores began to save scores of families. Per’s Mary, John’s mother, where was she? Pages of tears, faith, fear, connection.

Poignantly, Per wrote, 'Your courage was my courage. I will never stop hoping to see you again'.

His writings revealed that during the missions some fishing vessels had been lost and, as Mary had not returned, he feared she'd gone down with one of them.

'I tried.' Per penned finally.

John closed the journal one last time and secured it with its tattered tie.

It was time.

"Well father, our last supper." John plated the feast and ate, carefully savouring the flavours.

It was difficult to imagine the enormity of such heroic activities, far beyond his eye. He laid his father by a lone tree, while John opened the knife and carved into its bark the initials P and M, only separated by a heart.

He leaned towards his father's casket, lain inside a hand-carved Viking galley, a fitting representation of his father's beloved heritage. He watched as the sun moved west and had almost descended on the incoming waters. The tide soon lapped over the foy, reclaiming it.

As the orange sun touched the horizon, John lowered the precious sunset-drenched galley into the North Sea waves. He encouraged its onward journey with a tender push.

“Go be with her,” he whispered.

# Malcolm

## by Louise Crosbie

I can't see Malcolm, but I can hear him.

He's always there, murmuring at times, barely audible. On other occasions he is very insistent and not at all easy to ignore, louder and louder, until the shrillness of his tone reverberates around my skull. I can't remember when Malcolm moved in, maybe he's always been there.

Some days I get out of bed. The clothes from yesterday, the same ones as the day before that, are the easiest to put on. The room is dark and smells stale. Boxes lie discarded on the floor, bottles clink under my feet. Malcolm stirs in my pocket. He can move from one pocket to another; hoodies to jeans, ever present.

Looking in the mirror, I don't recognise the face that peers back. My limbs feel heavy and disordered, brushing hair or teeth feels beyond my motor skills, so I don't bother. The effort of thinking is equally laborious, thoughts move like treacle to formulate actions.

"We're not going out!" he suddenly shouts. Somehow, he knows my thoughts before I have them. "Remember what happened last time?" His tone peevish and irritable.

Do I need to go somewhere today? Do I have to see someone?

"But we can't go out, they will look at you."

"Shhhhh Malcolm," I placate.  It's best not to get him angry.

"But we know you don't like people looking at you," he snaps, never missing an opportunity for an additional jab.

Malcolm is not kind, but he is not wrong. Almost immediately I'm ten years old again, surrounded by a group of people, all staring. The faces are always blurred and indistinct, the words less so. No, no, no don't go there, not today. Anxiety claws at my stomach and my mouth feels dry, always so dry these days.

I read the card I picked up from the bedside table. I have an appointment on the other side of town. It was important; someone said so. I'll need to get a bus, but I don't like buses, full of so many people, staring. Maybe

I won't go. Why was it important? My brain moves so slowly, fogged by the vodka I drink to try and shut Malcolm up.

It's bright outside, the sunlight scorching the back of my eyes. I blink repeatedly but can't focus. Walking to the bus stop is an effort; my legs feel disjointed and leaden. Malcolm continues to fume furiously in my pocket, intoning constantly. He doesn't like when I don't do what he says. It's much easier to agree with him.

The bus comes, and I get on, scrabbling in pockets to find change for the fare. The driver taps the steering wheel impatiently, and Malcolm complains bitterly. Slumped in the nearest seat, anxiety washes over me in increasing waves. My breathing quickens and I feel clammy. There are so many people in here, all staring. I pull up my hood and clasp it tightly around my head. Moaning to myself, I rock rhythmically. Block out the people, block out Malcolm.

"What's wrong with that man, Mummy?" a child says.

"Shhhh – don't stare."

"But why is he doing that?"

"I don't know. Let's move over here."

I peer out and I'm met by the full, frank gaze of the curious child, before she is quickly moved to a seat much further away from me. The eye contact is unblinking and laced with fascinated revulsion.

"She's looking at you, I told you that would happen! I told you! I told you! You just don't listen to me!" Malcolm screeches. On and on he goes, repeating and repeating, a cacophony in my head.

"Shut up, shut up, just shut up please Malcolm!" I whisper.

Reasoning never works. I rock faster and faster, trying to silence the ringing in my head. So much noise, I can't think. More people on the bus turn to look at me and Malcolm sneers triumphantly. I can't stand this, I've got to get out, got to get out of here. I ring the bell. The wave of relief from the other passengers is palpable, lifting me up and carrying me off the bus.

I stop outside what I think is the address on the card. How did I get here?

"Don't go in there. Are you even listening to me?"

He is furious now. I can almost feel the spit-flecked

vitriol of his anger on my face. My brain feels like it could crack my skull wide open, any moment, spilling out.

"Shut up Malcolm! Shut up! Just SHUT UP!"

I suddenly wonder if Malcolm lives in my pocket, or do I live in his? He's the one who is always in control. And with this thought I'm laughing hysterically. The sound is high-pitched, maniacal, and tears are pouring down my face. I slump against the wall and melt down onto the pavement. Perhaps if I lie here long enough, I will dissolve and disappear through the cracks. I shut my eyes; it's too bright. People just walk past. They're always staring, but they don't see me and now I'm invisible, just like Malcolm.

"Are you David?" asks a voice. It is blessedly quiet. That's not Malcolm's voice. Is it coming from my pocket?

"I don't know," I reply.

"You have our card in your hand and we were expecting a David today. Can I help you up?"

Inside is cool, calm and smells of lavender. The blinds are drawn, and the lights are muted, I can open my eyes. The voice belongs to a lady. It's soothing. She wants to talk to me. Why does she want to talk to me? No-one ever talks to me. She gives me tea and we sit in silence for a while.

"Who is Malcolm?" she asks eventually. "You mentioned him outside."

"Malcolm lives in my pockets, but maybe I'm in his? He will be furious if I talk to you."

"I see," says the quiet voice.

But how can she see? Everyone stares, but no-one ever sees.

"Well, we will come to Malcolm. But first I want to hear about you, David."

"You can't ignore Malcolm. He won't like it."

"Oh, I won't. But you're important too. Now, tell me about David first."

I don't know what to say. This feels strange, I am lying down in the cool, calm, lavender-scented room. Outside people are walking past.

For once, Malcolm is silent.

# The Winter of 1950
## by Jean Dickson

The icy cold wind felt like knives cutting into the bruises on his back. The snow was thick on the ground as Jamie tried to walk as fast as he could. His thin jacket just wasn't keeping the cold out, the elbows were threadbare, and you could see his thin jumper poking through it.

The years had not been kind to Jamie who was only 29 and looked so much older, but this was the life of a coalman. Each morning his back was breaking. It wasn't just at the weight of the bags that had to be carried up flights of stairs or down into cellars of the big houses. Sharp edges stuck out all over the bag. He wore a 'backing hat' as it was known, with a long piece of leather stitched on the back which hung down to protect his neck and shoulders. It seldom did.

"COAL MAN - COAL MAN." He heard a faint shout.

He stopped and looked back to see Mrs Stewart waving from the doorway of her small, terraced house, where she lived with her husband. She was a kind woman and always gave the delivery men a tip at Christmas, usually a bottle of stout and a fruit cake. He always shared his cake with his sister.

"Would you like to have this?" She held up a heavy dark green coat.

"Are you sure?" he said smiling. "Don't you want to keep it as it was ..."

She stopped him before he could finish. "No definitely not - it's gathering dust. I'd rather it went to good use."

"Well, if you're sure?" he smiled.

He thanked her and put it on immediately. It felt comfortable, like big arms around him.
She quickly turned and went inside; he was sure he could see tears in her eyes as she shut the door.

He walked home knowing his sister would be in before him. As soon as he opened the front door, he could smell the lentil soup coming from the stove.

She looked up. "New coat?"

He nodded and took off his hat and coat and hung them over the chair. A good wash at the kitchen sink was always the orders from his sister, before having their supper and chat about their day.

Afterwards, he decided to have a smoke before heading for bed. He pulled on his new coat again, fastened the buttons and turned the big collar up. This was the best coat he'd ever had. Outside it was still freezing, and the snow looked like it was going to fall again. He put his hand in the pocket and found an envelope. It was addressed to Miss Susan Abbey, 27 Alnwick Road.

He stared at it, then turned it over.

Sender - Corporal T Stewart 67984252, The Highland Light Infantry.

The envelope was sealed with no stamp on it. He shoved it back into the pocket. He knew Mrs Stewart had lost a son in the war. He never returned home after she waved him off. He felt a shiver go through his body. Should he take the letter back to the mother? It wasn't for her. Who was Miss Susan Abbey? A sweetheart perhaps? He decided to sleep on it.

He was up early and breakfasted and braved the walk to work, once again. A long day up and down stairs into cellars. Sometimes he'd be given some bread, meat, or a drink. Other days he'd get nothing.

Susan Abbey lived only four miles away. A good walk on a nice day. He decided that he would deliver it by hand on Sunday, his day off. It was still freezing cold, but he set off, wondering if he was crazy or doing the right thing. Something was pulling him to continue.

At last he was standing outside 27 Alnwick Road. It was a well-kept house with a tidy garden. The door had a polished brass handle and letter box. An elderly lady answered his knock on the door.

“Good afternoon. My name is Jamie Hughes and I’m looking for Miss Susan Abbey, he said nervously. “I found a letter for her and wanted to deliver it in person.”

Jamie handed the envelope to the lady. She took it and quickly turned it over to see the sender’s name.

“Corporal T Stewart,” she said, her hand shaking.

“Susan is my daughter,” she said, sounding emotional. “You’d better come in and tell me how you found this letter please?”

Jamie explained about the gifted coat and discovering the letter was inside.

"Susan will be home from work soon," Mrs Abbey went on to say. "We are so proud of her. She's in the Woman's Patrol; one of the first in this area. Keeping an eye on the women at the factories and hostels. Some of their behaviour would make your toes curl, I tell you."

He heard a key in the door.

"Come to the front room, Susan!" her mother called.

"This is Jamie, and he has a letter that belongs to you." Susan looked a little taken aback. She was tall, slim and wore her uniform and a tired but fresh face. They didn't have many visitors and letters were few and far between.

Mrs Stewart handed her daughter the envelope. She took it and read the address; it was obvious that she recognised the writing straight away.

"It's been seven years since I've received a letter from Tommy," she said almost talking to herself. She carefully opened it.

"Dear Susan, As I place pen to paper..." She stopped reading aloud.

"Will you excuse me, please?" she cried and walked

quickly out of the room.

"Will I make you some tea, Jamie? You must have come a long way," asked Mrs Abbey.

She returned shortly with tea, homemade scones, and jam.

Jamie drank the last of his tea. "I need to be going as it's a long walk home."

Susan walked back into the front room, holding the letter folded and returned safely in its envelope.

"I would like to thank you so much for bringing this letter to me."

"It was no bother at all. I felt as it was unopened, I had to deliver it to you," Jamie said starting to leave.

"Let me walk you to the door, Jamie," Susan smiled.

"I hope it's not been too upsetting getting the letter after all this time?" asked Jamie as he stood out in the cold. He wasn't looking forward to the long walk back home.

"It's been fine and really it's given me closure. The war

has had devastating effects on every family."

In the following weeks, he could not get Susan Abbey out of his mind. Maybe if they had met in different circumstances, he wondered. He knew she worked near the hostels, so he had nothing to lose. On his next day off, he decided he would walk around the area he knew she would be.

He was just about to give up and walk back home when he heard a familiar voice.

"Hello, Jamie. It's so nice to see you."

He turned around. "Great to see you too, Susan!" he smiled.

# The Awakening
## by Steven Easton

I woke up slowly in a warm bed in a room that I did not recognise. A door opened and I sat up pulling the duvet tighter to my chest. A young lady quietly entered and asked me to dress and make my way through to the next room. She saw my confusion and pointed to the corner before turning and leaving, quietly closing the door behind her.

A small wooden chair sat in the corner with a pile of neatly folded clothes and a pair of shoes placed on top. Although the clothes were not mine, they felt comfortable, and the shoes fit well. Hesitant at first, I opened the door and stepped out where the lady motioned to follow her down a long, narrow corridor. Her steps echoed across the flagstones. I reached out to feel the oak panels lining the passage from the bedroom to a single door at the other end, with nothing in between. The lady stopped and instructed me to proceed.

“What is this?” I asked.

“Please continue through,” she replied.

I opened the door and paused. I could see a large empty room ahead and glanced back.

“Please continue through,” the lady repeated. “There is nothing to fear.”

The room was circular and very large, with many doors all the way round. As I began to count them, they started to open, one by one, and from each one, a person stepped through and looked around. Once all the doors had closed, we all turned to face each other.

“What is this?” I asked the man standing next to me.

“I don’t know,” he replied. “I just woke up and was led here.”

On my left, a young woman stood trembling. She muffled her splutters with her sleeve as her tears drenched her cheeks. She wore the same clothing as me, a plain white tunic with a single pocket at the front.

"Who are you?" I asked her.

"I'm … I'm … I don't know … I can't remember." She looked puzzled.

"Where are you from?"

"I don't know," she replied, wiping her tears again. "Who are you?"

My eyes scanned the others as I searched my mind. I knew who I was. Didn't I? But I couldn't answer her. My name was there in front of me but then gone before I could grasp it. It was a teasing thought dancing evasively around my skull, just beyond comprehension, hiding in a mind enveloped by thick, wet fog.

A larger door opened, and we were all led to a grand hall, like a ballroom. It too was lined in aged oak throughout. Intricate plasterwork detailed the ceiling in great swirls, sweeping and spiralling in a crescendo towards the centre, crowned by a majestic and brilliant chandelier. The centrepiece hung imposingly above us, radiant and sparkling, drawing me close, so bright that it appeared to cast its light beyond the hall itself.

A man entered and walked confidently to the centre of the room. He was the eldest in the room by far, and much older than anyone I had ever seen before. He was very tall, and walked with purpose and vigour, projecting a vibrancy in his stride that drew all eyes upon him. The Elder stood directly below the chandelier, casting no shadow, bathed in warmth as the luminescence draped over him.

“Please gather round,” the Elder said with gentle resolve. He wore a plain white tunic, identical to ours. He stood surveying the room. His gaze swept across us like a lighthouse beacon flashing the horizon, stopping at me momentarily, his beam intensifying in my pupils, calling my ship back on course. “Please gather round,” he repeated firmly.

We all shuffled forward a few paces to the centre and I was now embedded in the middle of the group.

“Don’t be scared. You won’t come to harm here,” he said.

"Where are we?" asked a voice nervously from behind.

"You are in a safe place," the Elder replied.

"What do you want with us?" called another.

"We would like you to settle a matter that is very important to us," the Elder explained.

I looked around and we shared a similar puzzled expression.

"You have been brought here to complete a series of tasks."

"Why us?" another voice called out, this time loud and aggressive. It was the man standing next to me. He was frightened.

The Elder continued. "You have been selected and brought here because you can help us. You all live together in society. You do not know each other but you all come from the same place. Some of you are wealthy, while others are poor. Some of you have inherited your riches over many generations while others have earned every penny.” He paused as if to let his words sink in.

“Some of you are young, while others are old. Some of you are married with families, while others have no family at all. Some of you have disabilities and challenges. Some of you are clever and highly educated, while some of you are clever and poorly educated. Some of you are not clever at all.”

“You don’t know anything about me!” the man yelled.

“Silence!” the Elder commanded. The hall fell to a silence which hung heavy in the air.

“There are different colours of skin here today, and different attitudes present in this room. Your religious views and belief systems differ vastly, and a plethora of cultures exist that both complement and clash with each other,” the Elder carried on.

“Some of you have been given many chances to live a meaningful life while others have been deprived of any chance at all. Each of you possesses skills and merits that are distinctive to your own self. Likewise, you each possess faults. You have individual preferences and dislikes. You are unique."

He paused and looked deeply into my eyes, raising his arm, and pointed a long bony finger towards me.

"You all have something in your pocket."

He was right, I could feel something at the front of my tunic. I put my hand in the pocket and felt a small piece of paper, neatly folded with sharp corners, the paper heavy and textured like linen.

"On that paper is the answer to the first task I am about to set you."

I unfolded it and looked at it.

"You have one task for today, and that is to decide who you are."

I looked again at the paper. It was blank.

# The Jacket
## by Lorraine Johnston

It's been through the wars, literally. First Bosnia, then Iraq. Luckily, I wasn't fit for Afghanistan. I'm not fit for much these days.

Seems I've never been 'fit for purpose'.

I managed home on leave for the wee one's first round of Chemo. I didn't make it home for her second, or her last. Emily lost her fight in her mother's arms with me elsewhere fighting someone else's war.

I wasn't there for my wife or my wee girl. All I had left of them, was my wedding ring looped onto my dog tags and Emily's favourite blue marbles she'd given me before I went on tour. "Bring them back safe Daddy," were her last words to me, wrapped in a chocolate-smelling hug with sticky fingers on my neck.

I can still smell that hug now.

I wasn't there at home, and I wasn't there on tour.

I wasn't with them when they triggered the IED.

I wasn't with a radio when they needed the medics.

I couldn't return fire.

I froze.

I failed.

I failed them all.

Back on home territory, I couldn't get a job. I lost my married quarters along with my marriage. I lost my flat because of rent arrears and then ended up in a homeless shelter for 2 nights, then another 2, until my night terrors made me unwelcome.

I didn't own much. Finding food and staying warm and dry became my daily mission. My boots had been stolen at the shelter and now all I had was cheap trainers; useless for keeping trench foot at bay.

The weight of grief and trauma is a lot to carry. It hurt so much that I was numb. I tried to remain orderly and organised. My right pocket was filled with things of the present and my left pocket was filled with the past.

Right pocket – interview haircut voucher, Food Bank card, Counsellor's card, Samaritans Card, Helpline Card, Social Worker's card, dead Davey's Methadone card, penknife and £4.11. No phone.

Left Pocket – Wedding ring, dog tags, my General Service and Operational Service medals, a small stick whittled into the shape of a dragon and my most treasured items of all, Emily's precious marbles.

My jacket had been washed, scrubbed, and bleached several times over to get rid of the detritus of war. Bloody stains that refused to go away. I'd been offered a new one, but this was the last thing Emily hugged and I could never part with that.

I kept myself to myself. I fashioned a bedspace from whatever dry cardboard I could find from the shop skips, and I'd de-camp in the early hours before the public could come out and be offended.

I'd lost my dignity and respect years ago. I'd spent too many cold and long nights alone with my own thoughts. Flashbacks of explosions and being under fire, would be triggered by a tyre blowing out or fireworks being used in someone else's celebration. The regular monument homeless guy would sit and stare at me. It reminded me of the feeling when a sniper's sight homed in on my epaulette.

I was twitchy and on edge all the time which must have made me appear insane. But I was acutely aware of everything, everywhere, all the time.

Sleep was never deep and if there was any noise, I would awaken already knowing what had made it. My memory bank had all potential hazards filed between the folds of my brain, never to be redacted. Fox screams in the wee small hours or hedgehogs rustling in the dried leaves. Shop shutters being rolled up to start a new day. Glass bottles being tipped out of the back of the pub and chink-smashing into the recycling bin. Footsteps accompanied by the lighter click clicks of the dog's claws on the pavement. Groups of young men, stinking of pumped-up adrenalin and boredom, gunning for a fight. All noises registered instantly as they were created.

Until the 11th of November.

The council workers had tidied gardens at the cenotaph and planted specially commissioned metal poppies on long sticks, pushed into the strip of lawn in preparation. The police had cordoned off the side streets to allow for the dignitaries and various military and civilian processions to arrive and people were claiming their position as close to the cenotaph as they were allowed.

We'd all been cleared from our usual sleeping spots, but I managed to get some space on my own, next to the bridge. I had a clear view of it all, could hear the lone piper and was far enough away to salute my respect for my colleagues and not have my tears seen by others.

As soon as it was over, people left as quickly as they'd arrived. They'd paid their dutiful two minutes of respect.

As the last remaining people pulled away from their stoic stances and started to think about the rest of their day, a young woman arrived, holding a little boy's hand. He was wearing a child sized DPM jacket and had one hand in his pocket. He was staring down at the rows of poppy wreathes and flowers. She placed a single rose on the step and then ruffled her son's hair with love.

The lad rummaged around his pocket for a few seconds and then took something out, kissed it and placed it on the rose. I couldn't make out what it was from the bridge, but it touched my heart in a place I thought had long since frozen over.

Late in the evening, after the drunks had gone home or been arrested, I picked up my rucksack and cardboard bed pack, and walked slowly over to the cenotaph. The rose petals had relaxed a little and I stooped down to see what had been placed there. I didn't see anything at first and then I saw an orange glint from the streetlight. There, inside the rose, was a single green marble, left there for his dad.

Tears streamed down my face, and something shifted. I felt a little bit lighter. It wasn't much, but just a little bit lighter. It felt like hope. Hope that had been missing for years. It was time I used that haircut voucher and made my Emily proud of her dad too

# Unfolding Truth
**by Pam J Kavanagh**

"Yes, it's time you had a walk. I'll grab my jacket and off we go." A crisp autumn morning walk through the fields will do us both good.

"Oh Barney, I've grabbed the wrong jacket," I sigh. I'm wearing Tom's and alarmingly it fits quite well. I need to cut down on the chocolate and wine.

Why does he keep all this rubbish in his pocket? Old parking and train tickets, cough sweets and what's this? I unfold a crumpled booking form for that trendy hotel he attended for a work conference a while back. He hasn't mentioned another conference. Perhaps he's surprising me for our anniversary. Barney suddenly tugs at his lead, snapping me out of my thoughts. For now, I just need to focus on not letting him disgrace himself with that bonny Black Labrador.

He did seem to get a lot out of that conference. He said he learned a lot, met some interesting new colleagues, and said the food was good too. He was the nearest to animated he's been in a long time. Do hope it's me who'll be going with him and not all his colleagues. It'll be a surprise for our twenty years of marriage. He's not usually romantic, so this will be a first. Perhaps he's improving with age like a fine wine which I'm about to cut down on or soon even his jacket won't fit me.

I'll check if I'm free over the anniversary weekend once I'm home. We could make a few days of it. Last time we did that, we were trying to repair the damage after the 'Susie event'.

Did it work? It helped a bit, but once trust has gone, things are rarely the same. There's always the small niggling doubt in the back of your mind. I wonder what happened to Susie. She very nearly succeeded in whisking him away, but the guilt of abandoning Harry and Lucy, who were little more than toddlers at the time, proved too much for him to carry out his escape plan to her Somerset flat.

I jump as his mobile phone starts to ring. Which pocket is it in?

"Hello, this is Mia, Tom's wife," I answer. "He's left his mobile at home and he's at work. Who's speaking please?" There is a hesitation. "Oh, Michael, are you a colleague? You'll get him at work. He'll be very annoyed that he's left it behind. Ok, goodbye."

Well, he seemed a bit fazed to hear me and not Tom. I wonder which department he's in. He sounded quite a bit younger than us. I wonder if he's one of the 'interesting' new colleagues from the conference. It's always good to hear new ideas and developments of work projects. I'll phone Tom's secretary so he's aware that Michael needs to speak to him.

"Barney, get out of that mud right now; you are disgusting! Time to go home and hose you down."

Tom is a dear man really; I suppose I'm lucky. We have a good life together overall, and we still make each other laugh, which is a bonus.

I'll check my diary to see if I'm free over our anniversary weekend. That will be something to look forward to, presuming it's not a business event. I'll make sure I can still get into a pretty dress or two. I'm getting quite excited. He's a dark horse.

"Barney, get off that rug. You'll leave a muddy stain." That reminds me, I'll need to phone Lucy to see if she can look after you if we're going away.

"Hello Tom, didn't expect to see you before tea-time."

"Did I leave my mobile here?" he asks-nervously, or was that my imagination?

"Yes, it's here in your jacket pocket. I put on your jacket by mistake, silly me. Michael was trying to contact you. Have you time for a light lunch?"

The house phone interrupts us.

"Oh, can you answer the phone please, I'm still drying Barney?"

Tom comes back into the room, ashen-faced and trembling. He can hardly speak.

"Lucy's been in an accident, a head-on collision, we need to go to the hospital now!"

The journey passes in a blur, we can't think straight. "Just drop me here Tom and I'll run into A&E, and you park the car."

Lucy is being assessed when a nurse takes us to the unit. A consultant eventually emerges, takes us to a side room and tells us that her head injuries are serious. They are taking her straight to surgery. It could be several hours before they can tell us more and he advises us to go home, saying they'll do everything they can and assuring us that the surgical team is excellent.

We drive home in silence and tears trickle down my face. I reach down into the pocket and find nothing more useful than cough sweets. I've done it again. No surprises this time. How life has changed since this morning.

As soon as I'm home I phone Harry who is devastated to learn about his twin sister. He says he'll drive straight here. Tom phones a few friends. When Harry arrives, we have a group hug and weep.

The consultant phones late at night to say Lucy has come through the surgery but the next few days are critical, and that she has been put into a medically induced coma. We take it in turn to sit by her bed and gaze anxiously at her beautiful head, swathed in bandages and tubes, and at all the machinery beeping and flashing and displaying numbers which mean little to us.

Several days pass and I arrive to let Tom go home and get some sleep. He takes my hand gently, looks me full in the face and says "I'm so sorry, Mia, the strain of all this has brought matters to a head. Michael is coming to pick me up and take me back to his home where I'll be living from now on."

I stand looking at him, unable to speak.
"You, Harry, and Lucy will always be my family, but I realise I can't live without Michael. I'm so, so sorry, Mia. You did nothing wrong. You have nothing to reproach yourself with."

He has nothing more to say so he leaves.

I sink into the visitor's chair next to Lucy, pulling my cardigan close to me and I reach into the pocket and pull out one folded-up tissue.

Printed in Great Britain
by Amazon

70980156R00037